Published in 2010 by Windmill Books, LLC
303 Park Avenue South, Suite # 1280, New York, NY 10010-3657

Adaptations to North American Edition © 2010 Windmill Books

Published in 2006 by Autumn Publishing,
A division of Bonnier Media Ltd,
Chichester, West Sussex, PO20 7EQ, UK.
© 2006 Autumn Publishing

CREDITS:
Author: Sarah Nash
Illustrator: Andy Everitt-Stewart

Publisher Cataloging Data

Nash, Sarah
    Scaredy Bear / written by Sarah Nash ; illustrated by Andy Everitt-Stewart.
        p. cm. – (Stories to grow with)
    Summary: Amy and her stuffed animal friends share their fears and promise to help each other overcome them.
    ISBN 978-1-60754-472-2 (lib.) – ISBN 978-1-60754-473-9 (pbk.)
ISBN 978-1-60754-474-6 (6-pack)
    1. Fear—Juvenile fiction 2. Teddy bears—Juvenile fiction 3. Toys—Juvenile fiction [1. Fear—Fiction 2. Teddy bears—Fiction
3. Toys—Fiction] I. Everitt-Stewart, Andy II. Title III. Series
    [E]—dc22

Manufactured in the United States of America.

For more great fiction and nonfiction, go to windmillbooks.com.

Scaredy Bear

Written by Sarah Nash
Illustrated by Andy Everitt-Stewart

alphabet
s o u p ™

an imprint of
WINDMILL BOOKS ™
New York

Scaredy Bear had long golden fur that was the color of summer sunshine.
He had velvet-soft paws.
And he had a secret fear that made him quiver and quake when little girls were nearby.

One evening Scaredy Bear heard a noise.
He crept to the edge of his shelf.
He could see a giant blanket beehive below.
Was the noise coming from inside?

OOOPPPS!

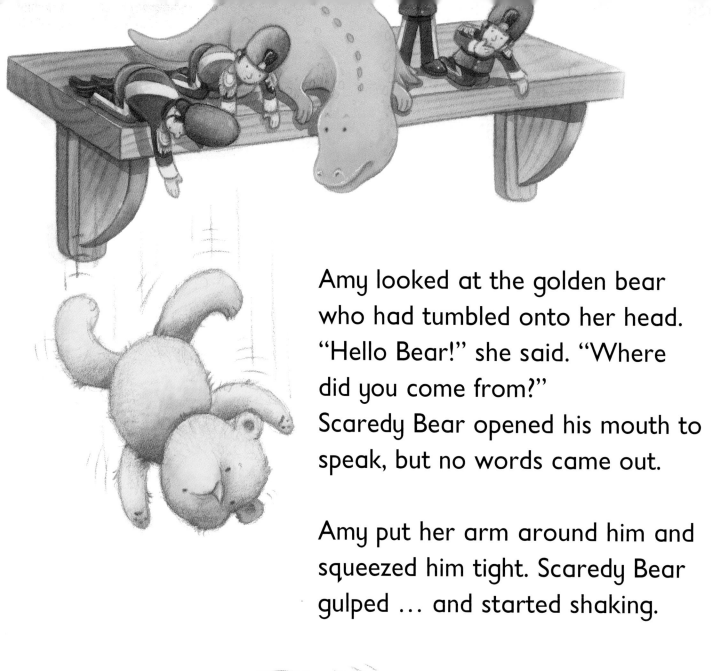

Amy looked at the golden bear
who had tumbled onto her head.
"Hello Bear!" she said. "Where
did you come from?"
Scaredy Bear opened his mouth to
speak, but no words came out.

Amy put her arm around him and
squeezed him tight. Scaredy Bear
gulped ... and started shaking.

"Come and join us. My name's Amy. What's your name?"
Amy leaned down and looked into Scaredy Bear's eyes.

His fur shivered...

... his nose quivered...

... and his eyes filled with tears.

"Scaredy Bear,"
he whispered.

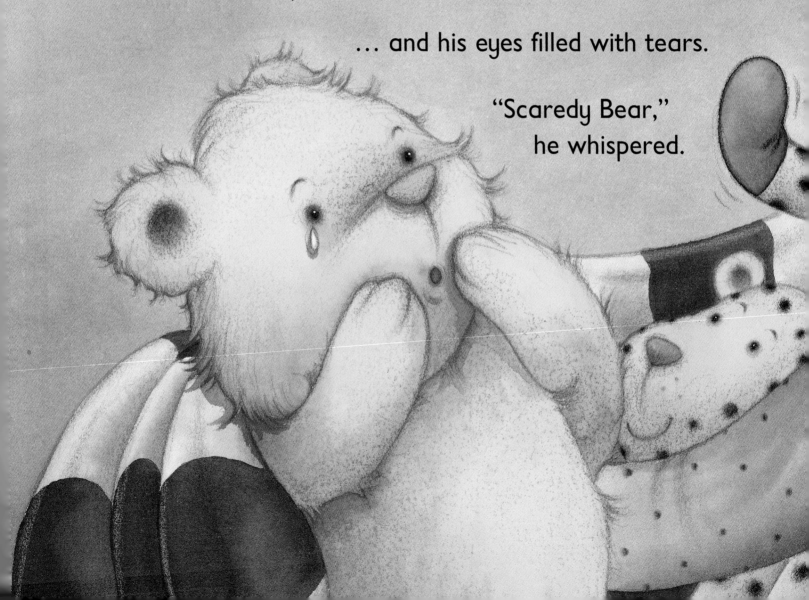

"What are you scared of?" asked Amy.
Scaredy Bear opened his mouth, but no sound came out.

"Daddy says everyone is scared of something," said Amy. "But if you can say what it is, then people will help you to stop being scared. We all have something that scares us."

Amy reached out to her elephant.

"Trunky's scared that someone will tie a knot in his trunk … we'll untie it for you!"

Scaredy Bear
watched all the
other animals nodding
their heads in agreement.

Amy reached out to take her leopard in her arms.

"Spot's scared that his spots will come off in the wash ... we won't let your spots wash off!"

The animals all shook their heads fiercely.

Amy braided her dolly's long blond hair.

"Flower's scared someone will cut her hair and she won't be beautiful anymore."

Scaredy Bear watched as Flower's eyes filled with tears.

"We'll think you are beautiful whatever your hair is like," said Amy.
Flower smiled and brushed her tears away.

"Zippy's scared someone will hide him and he'll be lost forever," continued Amy.
"NEVER!" chorused the animals.

"We'll all look and look and look and never give up until we find you," said Amy.
All the animals nodded and smiled.

Amy stroked Kitty's soft fur and kissed her nose.

"Kitty's scared her whiskers will fall out
and I won't love her anymore."

She gave Kitty a big hug.
"I'll love you even if you have NO whiskers,"
she promised.

"Scaredy Bear, it's your turn now. Tell us, what are you scared of?"
"I'm scared of little girls," gulped Scaredy Bear. "They might pull out my fur and rip my stitching."
"I'm a little girl," said Amy, "And I promise I will NEVER rip your stitching or pull out your golden fur."

Scaredy Bear looked at her. She wasn't scary.

He gave Amy a smile.
He felt warm and comfortable and ...

... not scared at all!

"But what are you scared of, Amy?" asked Scaredy Bear.
"I'm scared of being alone," Amy answered.
"You're not alone!" shouted her friends. "WE'RE HERE!"

"Then I'm not SCARED anymore," said Amy.
"Come and live with us and we'll all help each other...
then you won't be a Scaredy Bear anymore!"